NEVER TEASE
A WEASEL

by Jean Conder Soule
illustrated by Denman Hampson

PARENTS' MAGAZINE PRESS
NEW YORK
© Copyright 1964 by Parents' Magazine Press
A Division of Parents' Magazine Enterprises, Inc.
Library of Congress Catalog Card Number 64-12353.

You can knit a kitten mittens
And perhaps that cat would purr.
You could fit a fox with socks
That exactly matched his fur.

You could make a goat a coat
With a collar trimmed in mink;
Or give a pig a wig
In a dainty shade of pink.

But never tease a weasel;
This is very good advice.
A weasel will not like it
And teasing isn't nice!

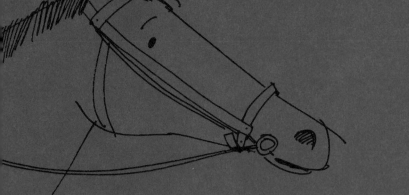

You could make a riding habit
For a rabbit if you choose;

Or make a turkey perky
With a pair of high-heeled shoes.

You could make a collie jolly
With a gay crocheted cravat;

Or make a possum blossom
In an Easter Sunday hat.

But never tease a weasel,
Not even once or twice.
A weasel will not like it
And teasing isn't nice!

You could build a mouse a house
With a chimney made of bricks.

You could give a dove some gloves
And a set of walking sticks.

But never tease a weasel.
There! Now I've said it thrice.
A weasel will not like it—
And teasing isn't nice!

You could give a mule a pool
And some jaunty swimming trunks;

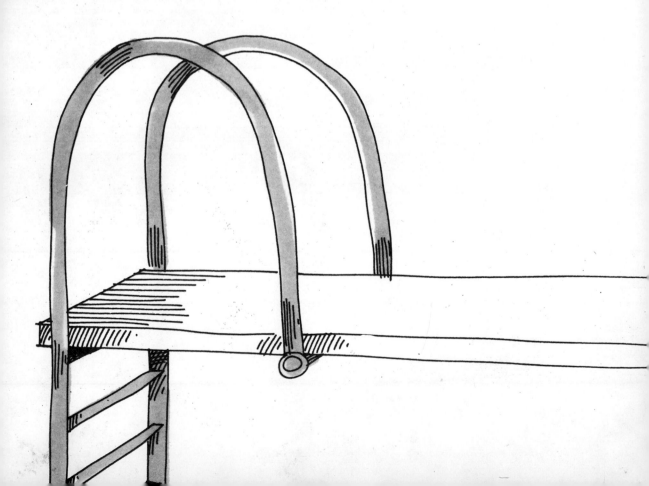

Send a case of Spanish lace
To a pair of lady skunks.

You could give a fish a dish
For her favorite seaweed stew;

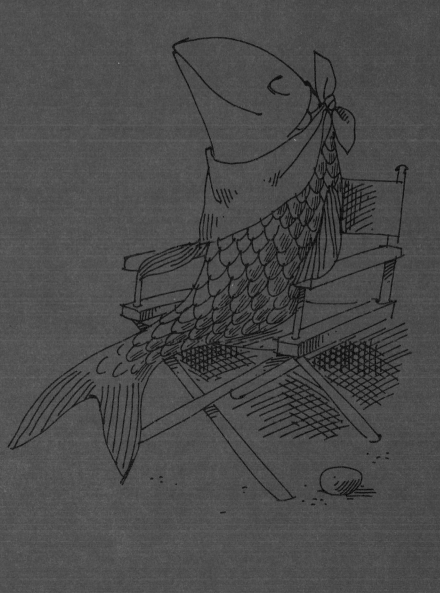

Send three frogs some sailing togs
And a yachting cap or two.

But never tease a weasel.
Now I can't be more precise.
A weasel will not like it,
And teasing isn't nice!

You could bake a drake a cake
For his special birthday treat;

You could braid a bug a rug
To make his bug house neat.

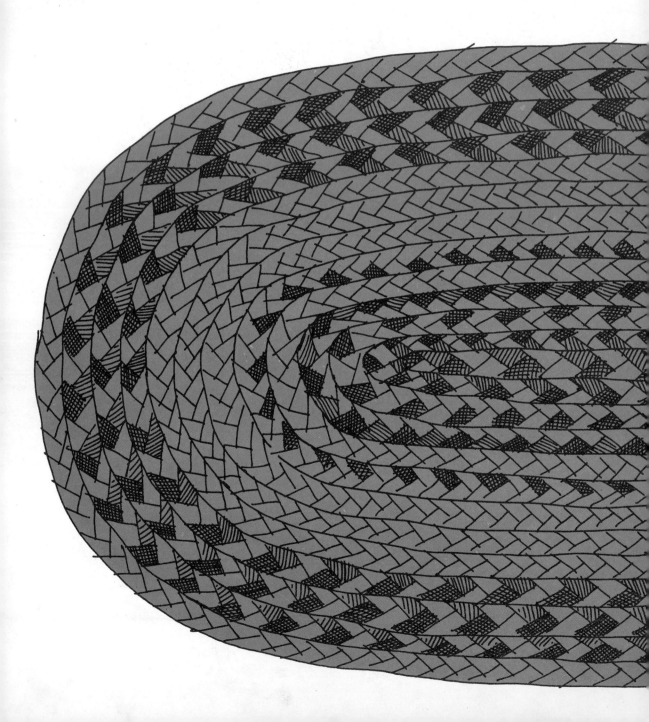

You could feed a spider cider
Or perhaps pink lemonade;

Or give a moose some juice
To sip on in the shade.

But never tease a weasel.
Now remember what I've said!
It's more fun to please a weasel
And be friends with him instead.